W9-AXY-338

APR 5 1993

EVERETT ANDERSON'S YEAR

EVERETT ANDERSON'S YEAR

by LUCILLE CLIFTON

illustrations by ANN GRIFALCONI

HENRY HOLT AND COMPANY • *New York*

Published by Henry Holt and Company, Inc.,
115 West 18th Street, New York, New York 10011.
Published simultaneously in Canada by
Fitzhenry & Whiteside Ltd.,
91 Granton Drive, Richmond Hill, Ontario L4B 2N5.
First published in 1974 by Holt, Rinehart and Winston.
Reissued in 1992 by Henry Holt and Company.

Library of Congress Cataloging-in-Publication Data
Clifton, Lucille.
    Everett Anderson's year / by Lucille Clifton; illustrated by Ann
Grifalconi.
    Summary: Chronicles, in verse, the month-to-month activities of
seven-year-old Everett Anderson throughout the seasons of the year.
    ISBN 0-8050-2247-3
    [1. Family life—Fiction. 2. Seasons—Fiction. 3. Afro-
Americans—Fiction. 4. Stories in rhyme.] I. Grifalconi, Ann,
ill. II. Title.
PZ8.3.C573Ex 1992
[E]—dc20   92-4683

Printed in the United States of America
on acid-free paper. ∞

10 9 8 7 6 5 4 3 2 1

JANUARY

"Walk tall in the world,"
says Mama
to Everett Anderson.
"The year is new and
so are the days,
walk tall in the world,"
she says.

FEBRUARY

Everett Anderson
in the snow
is a specially
ice cream boy to know
as he jumps and calls
and spins and falls
with his chocolate nose and
vanilla toes.

MARCH

What if a wind
would blow a boy
away,
where would he go
to play?
What if a wind
would blow him back
next day,
what would his
Mama say?
This time instead of
run outside
Everett Anderson thinks
he'll hide.

APRIL

Rain is good
for washing leaves
and stones and bricks and
even eyes,
and if you hold
your head just so
you can almost see
the tops of skies.

MAY

Remember the time we took a ride
to the country and saw a horse and a cow,
and remember the time I picked a weed
and Daddy laughed and laughed real loud,
and remember he spanked me for throwing stones?
I wish it could be like that now,
thinks Everett Anderson when he's alone.

JUNE

In 14A, till Mama comes home
bells are for ringing
and windows for singing
and halls are for skating
and doors are for waiting.

JULY

Everett Anderson thinks he'll make
America a birthday cake
only the sugar is almost gone
and payday's not till later on.

AUGUST

Now I am seven Mama can stay
from work and play with me all day.
I'll teach her marbles and rope and ball
and let her win sometimes, and all
our friends will be calling each other and saying
Everett Anderson's Mama and him are playing.

SEPTEMBER

I already know where Africa is
and I already know how to
count to ten and
I went to school every day last year,
why do I have to go again?

OCTOBER

Don't run when you see
this terrible monster
with a horrible nose and
awful eyes,
under those jaggedy
monstery teeth
it's Everett Anderson
in disguise!

NOVEMBER

Thank you for the things we have,
thank you for Mama and turkey and fun,
thank you for Daddy wherever he is,
thank you for me, Everett Anderson.

DECEMBER

"The end of a thing
is never the end,
something is always
being born like
a year or a baby."

"I don't understand,"
Everett Anderson says.
"I don't understand where
the whole thing's at."

"It's just about Love,"
his Mama smiles.
"It's all about Love and
you know about that."

ABOUT THE AUTHOR AND ILLUSTRATOR

LUCILLE CLIFTON, poet, storyteller, college professor, mother of six and grandmother of four, is the author of many books for young readers. Seven of her picture books with Henry Holt feature Everett Anderson, including *Everett Anderson's Goodbye* (a Coretta Scott King Award winner), *Everett Anderson's Nine-Month Long*, and *Everett Anderson's Christmas Coming*.

Ms. Clifton lives in Maryland.

ANN GRIFALCONI, a native New Yorker, is the author and illustrator of *The Village of Round and Square Houses* and *Darkness and the Butterfly*. As an illustrator, she has collaborated with many writers on several picture books, including five Everett Anderson titles.